The Snowman™
AND THE SNOWDOG

based on characters created by
Raymond Briggs
and the story written by Hilary Audus and Joanna Harrison

PUFFIN

"Come on," called Billy to his old dog.
"We're here! Let's explore our new home."

But Billy's dog was too old and tired for exploring. As the months passed he became slower and slower, and then one day he died.

Together Billy and his mum buried him in the garden.

Winter came. Billy was lonely. He missed his old friend.

He had written a letter to Father Christmas and was about to take it downstairs when he tripped over a loose floorboard . . .

"What's this?" thought Billy as he pulled out an old shoebox. Inside he found a worn-out hat, some pieces of coal, a shrivelled tangerine and a tatty green scarf.

As Billy unfolded the scarf, an old photograph dropped
out. How odd! And then he realized. Another boy
had lived here and made an amazing snowman.

"I'm going to make a snowman too," thought Billy.
"Just like his one!"

He took the box
and ran outside,

and began to build
his *own* snowman.

He used two pieces of coal for the eyes and
a new tangerine for the nose . . .

and, last of all, he gave him a great big smile.
His Snowman was perfect.

But there was still
plenty of snow left.

Billy had an idea.
He started
building again . . .

and bit by bit, with two socks for ears, he made . . .

. . . a Snowdog!

Now it was late. Billy said goodnight
to his two new friends and went inside to bed.

At midnight, Billy was
woken by a muffled bark.

He peered out of the window and rubbed his eyes
in disbelief. Did the Snowdog move?

He ran downstairs and
flung open the back door.

And then the most magical
thing happened!

The Snowman and the Snowdog
came to life!

The Snowman politely shook his hand, and the Snowdog bounded up to say hello.

Then he was off up the garden where he
found the old dog's ball. He wanted to play!

But the Snowman had found something too.
It was a sledge.

Billy climbed on board. Out through the gate
they went, towards the park and up the hill.

When they reached the top,
Billy gasped in amazement.

The air was full of flying snowmen, rising up
from the gardens below. What a magical sight!

Suddenly the Snowman took Billy's hand and started to run.
Billy grabbed the Snowdog and before he knew it . . .

. . . they were **flying!**

Low over the rooftops they flew,

then high above the city

and out across the countryside . . .

All of a sudden the Snowman sneezed and his tangerine nose blew off.

They swooped down to find it, but when they landed they found something really exciting.

"Oh!" cried Billy. "An aeroplane!"

Together they went to take a closer look.

They climbed in and, with
the Snowman at the controls,
they were flying again.

Out to sea they flew, on and on
towards the North Pole . . .

And what a sight greeted them when they arrived.

There were snowmen a

They had all com

nowwomen **everywhere!**

o compete in *The Snowman's Annual Downhill Race!*

Billy and the Snowman reached the starting line just in time. The whistle blew and they were off!

Twisting and turning, they sped down the course. Soon Billy and the Snowdog were the only ones left, battling it out with a penguin.

And, just as it seemed certain the penguin would win, the little Snowdog stretched forward and broke the finishing-line tape with his nose.

They had
WON!

Amidst the celebrations,
Father Christmas arrived.
He handed Billy a small
parcel. "This is for you.
Happy Christmas!"

But there was no time to open the parcel . . .
Dawn was breaking and it was time to go.

When they landed in Billy's back garden
it was time for him to go back inside to bed.

"I wish you could come with me," said Billy, "but you
would melt indoors." Billy's eyes filled with tears.

He reached into his pocket for a hankie and instead found the present from Father Christmas.

Quickly he unwrapped it. Inside was a brand-new dog collar! He fastened it around the Snowdog's neck.

"There you are," he said. "Just like a proper dog!"

He turned to go, but as he did so the Snowdog's collar started to glow, brighter and brighter until suddenly . . .

"Woof!"
And where the Snowdog
had been was a real live
dog, his tail wagging
with delight!

"Oh!" cried Billy, scooping him up. "You're just what
I asked for in my letter to Father Christmas!"

Overjoyed, he hugged the Snowman,
and then it was time to go inside.

Back in his bedroom,
Billy waved goodnight
to the Snowman.

Then he snuggled down in bed with his new friend.

"I think I'll call you Socks," he said,
as he drifted off to sleep.

But when Billy woke up, Socks was nowhere to be seen. Billy's heart sank. Had it all been just a dream?

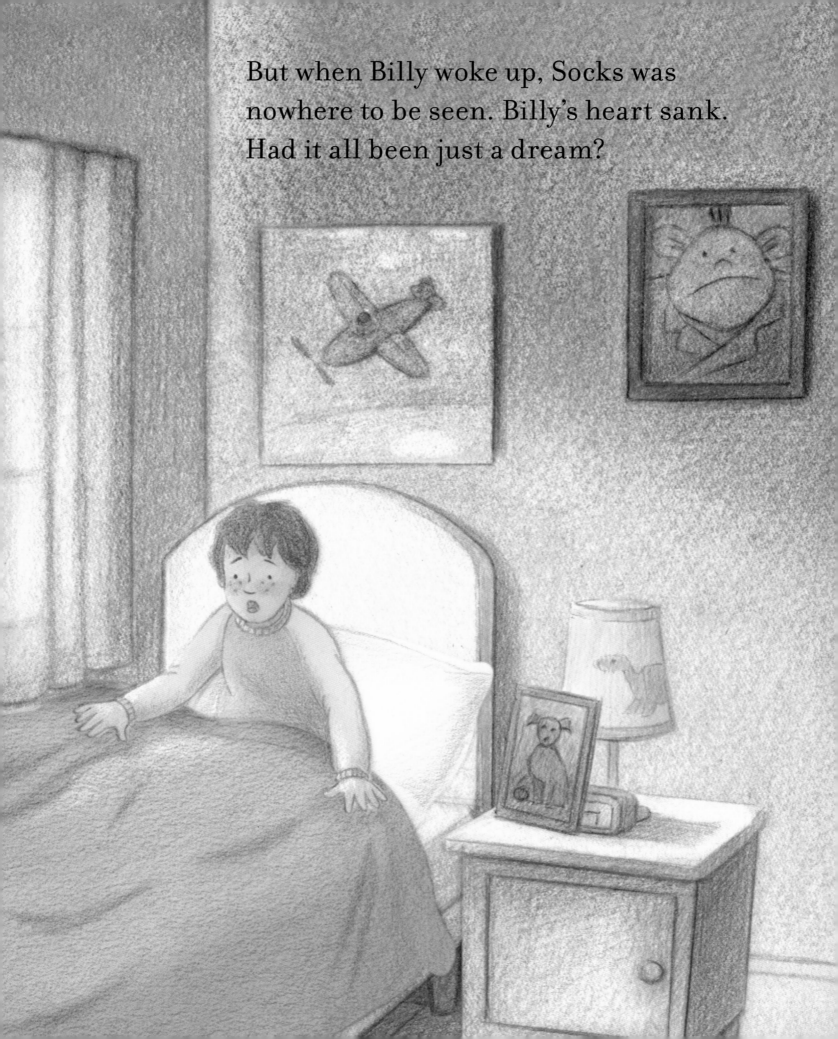

Then, hearing an excited bark, Billy rushed downstairs.
And there was Socks, waiting to go outside and play.

Billy opened the door and out Socks sped,
bounding towards the Snowman . . .

But the Snowman was gone,
melted away in the early morning sun.